## CARTER HIGH
### M Y S T E R I E S

# THE SECRET
# *Message*

By Eleanor Robins

SADDLEBACK
EDUCATIONAL PUBLISHING

# CARTER HIGH
## M Y S T E R I E S

SADDLEBACK
EDUCATIONAL PUBLISHING
www.sdlback.com

**Copyright ©2006, 2011 by Saddleback Educational Publishing**

ISBN-13: 978-1-61651-568-3
ISBN-10: 1-61651-568-6
eBook: 978-1-61247-136-5

Printed in Guangzhou, China
0812/CA21201201

16 15 14 13 12   2 3 4 5 6

# Chapter 1

Logan was at school. He walked down the hall. He was on his way to his locker. His friend, Drake, was with him.

Logan saw his friend, Willow. She was talking to a girl. Logan had never seen the girl before.

Logan asked, "Do you know that girl, Drake? The one who's talking to Willow?"

"No," Drake said.

"Have you ever seen her before?" Logan asked.

"No. She must be new here at Carter High," Drake said.

"Yeah. She must be. I think I'll go over

to them," Logan said. "And I'll find out who she is. I might want to ask her out."

"Why aren't I surprised?" Drake asked. Then Drake laughed.

Logan liked to date many girls. And Drake liked to joke with him about that.

"Talk to you later," Logan said.

"Okay," Drake said. Drake walked on down the hall.

Logan went over to Willow and the girl.

The girl said, "Good-bye, Willow." Then the girl hurried down the hall.

Logan asked, "Who's that girl? Is this her first day at Carter High?"

"Yes. Her name is Quinn. And she'll be in my math class," Willow said.

"I want to talk to her. I'll see you later, Willow," Logan said.

Then Logan hurried after Quinn. Logan was glad Quinn had to stop at her locker. Logan walked over to her. Logan said, "Hi. My name is Logan." He smiled. Then he asked, "Is this your first day at Carter High?"

"Yes," Quinn said.

"Do you know how to get to your first class?" Logan asked.

"No," Quinn said.

"Do you want me to show you where the class is?" Logan asked.

"No. I can find my own way," Quinn said. She shut her locker. Then she started to walk down the hall.

Logan started to go after her. But then he stopped. He was sure he would see her again. And he could talk to her then.

Logan walked on down the hall. He saw Drake. Drake was at his locker. His locker was next to Logan's locker.

Logan stopped at his locker. He got

his book for his first class. Drake got his book, too.

Then Logan and Drake walked to class.

Drake asked, "Who's the new girl? Where's she from?"

"Her name is Quinn. But I don't know where she's from," Logan said.

"I'm surprised you didn't walk her to her first class," Drake said.

"I asked her if she wanted me to show her where her class was. She said no. She said she could find her own way," Logan said.

Drake laughed. He said, "Too bad, Logan. But I know you. You won't give up. You'll talk to her again."

"Yeah. But first I have to see her again," Logan said.

The first bell rang.

"We need to get to class," Drake said.

"Yeah," Logan said.

The two boys hurried down the hall.

Logan was thinking about Quinn. How would he find her again? He couldn't just stand around her locker and hope he would see her again.

Logan and Drake got to their classrooms.

Drake said, "See you later."

"Yeah. See you later," Logan said.

Drake went into his class. And Logan went into his class.

Then Logan got a surprise. He saw Quinn. She was sitting in the front row. Maybe he could talk to her after class.

But Quinn stayed after class to talk to the teacher. So Logan didn't get a chance to talk to her.

# Chapter 2

It was the next week. Logan was at the bus stop. Drake was there, too.

Drake said, "I need to go to the gym before school this morning. Do you want to go with me?"

Logan said, "No. I want to get to my first class early today. So I'm going there as soon as I get off the bus."

"Why? Don't you have a test, Logan?" Drake asked.

"I want to talk to Quinn before school starts," Logan said.

"About what?" Drake asked.

"I'm not sure yet. But I might ask

Quinn for a date today," Logan said.

The bus arrived at the bus stop.

Logan and Drake got on the bus. Logan sat with Drake. They talked on the way to school. But they didn't talk any more about Quinn.

Soon the bus stopped in front of the school. Logan quickly got off the bus. Drake got off behind him.

"See you later, Drake," Logan said.

Then Logan went into the school. He hurried to his class. He wanted to be there when Quinn came.

But Quinn was already there. She was sitting at her desk. Logan walked over to her desk.

Quinn had a puzzle book. She was trying to break a code.

"Hi, Quinn. I see you like to break codes," Logan said.

Quinn looked up at Logan. She said,

"Yes. I do." Then she looked back down at the code.

"I like to break codes, too. The harder they are, the more I like them," Logan said.

But that wasn't true. Logan didn't think it was fun to try to break a code. So he had never wanted to try to break one before.

He wanted Quinn to think he liked codes. So maybe she would date him.

Quinn looked up at Logan again. Then she smiled.

Logan hoped Quinn would say something else to him. But she didn't.

But Quinn had smiled at him. So Logan thought she might date him now. And it might be a good time to ask her for a date.

"Carter High has a football game on Friday night," Logan said.

Quinn just looked at him. And she didn't say anything.

"Do you like football?" Logan asked.

"Yes," Quinn said.

But then she didn't say anything else to Logan. He wished Quinn would say something.

Maybe it was too soon to ask Quinn for a date. But Logan didn't want to wait. So he went ahead and asked her.

"Do you want to go to the game with me?" Logan asked.

"No," Quinn said. Then Quinn looked down at the code. And she didn't look back at Logan.

The bell rang. Logan hurried to his desk. He sat down.

Why didn't Quinn want to date him? Did she have a boyfriend?

Logan would find out. He would ask her as soon as class was over.

The class was okay. And the time went by quickly. But Logan was glad when the end of class bell rang.

Logan hurried over to Quinn. Quinn seemed surprised that he did.

Logan asked, "Do you have a boyfriend, Quinn?"

"Maybe," Quinn said. Then Quinn quickly picked up her books. And she hurried out of the room.

Quinn didn't say she would date him. And she didn't answer his question either.

But that was okay. Logan wanted to date her. And he wouldn't give up.

# *Chapter 3*

Logan walked out into the hall. But he didn't look for Quinn.

He saw Drake. Drake hurried over to talk to Logan.

"Did you talk to Quinn, Logan?" Drake asked.

"Yeah," Logan said.

"Did you ask her for a date?" Drake asked.

"Yeah," Logan said.

"What did she say? Is she going to date you?" Drake asked.

"No," Logan said.

Drake seemed surprised.

"Did she say why she won't date you?" Drake asked.

"No," Logan said.

"Maybe Quinn has a boyfriend," Drake said.

"Yeah. That's what I thought. So I asked her," Logan said.

"What did she say?" Drake asked.

"Maybe. That was all she said. Then she hurried out of the room. So maybe she has a boyfriend. And maybe she doesn't have one," Logan said.

Logan saw Willow. Drake saw her, too.

Drake said, "Willow is going too fast in her wheelchair again."

"Yeah. I hope a teacher doesn't see her," Logan said.

"Maybe Willow knows if Quinn has a boyfriend. Ask Willow," Drake said.

"Good idea. I'll ask her now," Logan said.

"Okay. See you at lunch," Drake said.

Drake walked down the hall.

Logan said, "Wait, Willow."

Willow stopped. And then she waited for Logan. Logan hurried over to Willow.

"Does Quinn have a boyfriend here? Or does she date someone at the school she came from?" Logan asked.

"I don't know. We've talked a few times. But it was only about homework," Willow said.

"I need you to do something for me," Logan said.

"Okay. What?" Willow asked.

"Ask Quinn if she has a boyfriend," Logan said.

"I think you should ask her that," Willow said.

"I did ask her. But she didn't tell me," Logan said.

Logan told Willow what Quinn said

to him. And he told Willow that he had asked Quinn for a date.

Then Willow said, "I can ask Quinn. But she might not tell me."

"Thanks, Willow. When do you think you'll ask her?" Logan asked.

"Quinn is in my next class. So I'll try to ask her then. And maybe I can tell you at lunch. I need to get to class now. I don't want to be late," Willow said.

Willow hurried down the hall. And she was going too fast again.

Logan went into his next class. The class was okay. But he was glad when the class was over.

He hurried out to the hall. And he looked for Willow. He wanted to know what she had found out.

Logan saw Willow. He hurried over to talk to her.

"Did you find out for me, Willow?

Does Quinn have a boyfriend or not?" Logan asked.

"No. She did have one at her other school. But they broke up when she moved here," Willow said.

Logan said, "Thanks for asking her, Willow. I wonder why she said no when I asked her for a date."

"I asked Quinn why. I hope it's okay with you that I did. But I thought you would want to know," Willow said.

Logan didn't know Willow was going to ask Quinn that. But he was glad Willow did.

"You're right about that, Willow. I do want to know. What did Quinn say?" Logan asked.

"She doesn't date boys she doesn't know. And she doesn't know you. So she told you no," Willow said.

"But she does know me. We're in the

same class," Logan said.

And he couldn't believe that was why Quinn said no.

"But Quinn still doesn't know you. I told her you and I are friends. But I'm not sure that will help you," Willow said.

"That was worth a try, Willow. Maybe she'll date me now. Thanks for telling her that we're friends," Logan said.

Logan hoped that would help him get a date with Quinn.

"See you at lunch," Willow said.

"Yeah," Logan said.

Willow went into a classroom.

Drake came up to Logan.

"Did you ask Willow? Does Quinn have a boyfriend?" Drake asked.

"Willow asked her. And Quinn said no," Logan said.

"So why did Quinn say she wouldn't date you?" Drake asked.

"Quinn told Willow that she doesn't know me. And she doesn't date boys she doesn't know," Logan said.

Drake seemed surprised.

"Why doesn't Quinn think she knows you? You're in her class, Logan," Drake said.

"Yeah," Logan said.

"Maybe she just told Willow that," Drake said.

"Yeah. Maybe," Logan said.

But Willow had told Quinn that she and Logan were friends. And maybe Quinn would date him now.

# Chapter 4

Later that day, Logan was on his way to lunch. Willow called to him.

She said, "Wait, Logan."

Logan stopped. Willow wheeled over to Logan. Then she gave him a note.

"What's this?" Logan asked.

"It's a message from Quinn," Willow said.

That surprised Logan.

"Quinn just gave that to me. She had lunch last period. And she wrote it during lunch," Willow said.

"Did you read it?" Logan asked.

"No. The message is for you. Not for

me. But Quinn said that you want to date her. And this is her answer."

He wanted to read the note before he had lunch with his friends. Logan quickly read the note. But Logan couldn't believe what he saw. Part of the note was in code…

Logan,

Willow told me that you're her friend. And I'd like to date you.

Do you want to talk about a date tomorrow?

I hope you do.

NFFU NF CFZPSF TDILPPM.

XF DBO NFFU JO GSPOU PG ULF TDILPPM.

XF DBO UBML BCPVU ULF EBUF ULFO.

Quinn

P. S. I'm glad you like to break codes as much as I do.

But Logan didn't like to break codes. He just told Quinn that to try to get a date with her. Logan wanted to break this code. But he didn't think he could do it. What was he going to do?

He would need some help. And he hoped his friends could help him.

Logan hurried into the lunchroom. He got his lunch. Then he looked for his friends.

Logan saw Drake and Willow. They were at a table. Paige was with them, too.

Logan hurried over to the table and sat down. Logan looked over at Willow. He asked, "Did you tell them?"

"No," Willow said.

"Did Willow tell us what?" Drake asked.

"Yes. What?" Paige asked.

"Willow gave me a note from Quinn," Logan said.

"Who's Quinn?" Paige asked.

"She is a new girl at Carter High. And surprise, surprise, Logan wants to date her," Drake said.

Then Drake laughed.

"What does the note say, Logan?" Paige asked.

"Yeah, Logan. What does the note say?" Drake asked.

"I don't know," Logan said.

"Why don't you know? Didn't you read the note?" Drake asked.

Logan said, "I tried to read the note. But Quinn wrote some of it in code."

The other three seemed surprised.

Logan looked at Willow. He asked, "Did you know Quinn wrote some of the note in code?"

"No. Quinn didn't tell me it was in code. And the message was for you. So I didn't look at it," Willow said.

"I would have," Drake said.

Logan thought Paige would have looked, too.

"Show us the note," Drake said.

"Yes. Show us the note," Paige said.

Logan gave the note to Drake. Drake looked at it. Then he gave it to Paige. Paige looked at the note. Then she gave it to Willow. Willow looked at the note. Then she gave it back to Logan.

Logan said, "I can't break this code. What am I going to do?"

"Don't worry about it. You don't have to break the code. You like to date lots of girls. Just date someone else. And forget about Quinn for now," Drake said.

Logan did like to date many girls. And he could always date someone else. But right now he wanted to date Quinn. So he had to break the code.

Logan said, "I have to break this code."

"Tell her you don't like to break codes," Drake said.

"I can't do that," Logan said.

"Why?" Willow asked.

"Yes, Logan. Why?" Paige asked.

"Quinn was trying to break a code before class. And I told her I liked to break codes, too," Logan said.

"You don't like to break codes. So why did you tell her that?" Drake asked.

"I was trying to get her to date me," Logan said.

Willow said, "It wasn't nice to lie to Quinn. So tell Quinn the truth, Logan. Tell her that you don't know how to break codes."

"I can't tell her that. She might not date me then," Logan said.

Drake said, "Tell Quinn the code is too hard for you. And then ask Quinn to help you break it. That wouldn't be a lie, Logan."

"Yeah. I could do that," Logan said.

Logan thought about that for a few more minutes. Then he said, "That's what I'll do. I'll tell Quinn the code is too hard for me. And I'll ask her to show me how to break it."

He would tell Quinn that tomorrow before class. And now he didn't have to worry about the code anymore.

# Chapter 5

It was the next morning. Logan sat on the bus. He was sitting with Drake. They were on their way to school.

"What are you going to do about the note?" Drake asked.

"I'll tell Quinn that the code is too hard. And then I'll ask her to help me break it," Logan said.

"That sounds like a plan to me," Drake said.

Soon the bus stopped in front of the school. The two boys got off the bus. Paige got off the bus behind them.

Drake said, "I see Quinn near the front door. Are you going over there now to talk to her?"

"Yeah. I might as well tell her now. And find out what she says," Logan said.

Paige came over to Logan and Drake.

"Did you break the code last night, Logan?" Paige asked.

Drake spoke before Logan could answer Paige.

"I need to talk to someone about my history homework. I'll see you later," Drake said.

Drake hurried off.

Logan said, "No, Paige. I didn't break the code. I knew I couldn't break it. So I didn't even try to break it."

"What are you going to do, Logan?" Paige asked.

Logan said, "I'll tell Quinn the code

is too hard. And I'll ask her to help me break it," Logan said.

"When will you tell her?" asked Paige.

"Quinn is near the front door. So I'll go over there now. And I'll tell her," Logan said.

Logan looked over at the front door. But he didn't see Quinn. She must have already gone to class.

"I want to find Quinn. So I'll talk to you later," Logan said.

"Okay," Paige said.

Logan went into the school. And he hurried to his first class.

He was right. Quinn was there. She was sitting at her desk. Logan walked over to her.

"Hi," Logan said.

Quinn was looking at a puzzle book. She was trying to break a code. Quinn didn't look up at Logan. She said, "I don't want to talk to you, Logan."

"Why? I thought you wanted to date me," Logan said.

"I said I don't want to talk to you," Quinn said.

"Why?" Logan asked again.

But Quinn didn't answer. And she didn't look up at him.

Logan was sure it was because of something Quinn wrote in the code. But what?

Logan had to break the code. He had to find out what it said. Then maybe Quinn would talk to him again. And maybe she would date him. But he knew he couldn't break it.

He would show the note to his friends again. One of them had to know how to break the code.

# Chapter 6

It was later the same day. Logan hurried into the lunchroom. He got his lunch. Then he looked for his friends.

Logan saw Drake, Paige, Willow, Jack, and Lin sitting at a table.

Jack and Lin lived at Grayson Apartments, too. And they knew Logan wanted to date Quinn. They had heard all about the note.

Logan went over to the table. And he sat down.

"What did Quinn say? Did she show you how to break the code?" Drake asked.

Logan said, "No. I didn't get to talk to

Quinn about the code. She didn't want to talk to me."

"Why?" Paige asked.

"Yes. Why?" Jack asked.

"I don't know. But Quinn is mad at me," Logan said.

"Why is Quinn mad at you, Logan?" Willow asked.

"Yeah. Why?" Drake asked.

"I think it's because of something she wrote in code. And I have to break that code. But I don't know how to break it," Logan said.

"Don't worry, Logan. We'll help you break the code," Willow said.

"Yeah," Drake said.

"Yes, Logan. We'll help. I like to break codes," Lin said.

"So do I. That's for sure," Jack said.

"Do you have the note with you, Logan?" Lin asked.

"Yes," Logan said.

"Maybe we can break the code after we eat lunch," Jack said.

"That sounds like a plan to me," Drake said.

All six started to eat and talk. But they talked too much. And it took them longer to eat lunch than they thought it would.

Then it was time to break the code.

"Are you ready to break the code?" Logan asked.

"Yeah," Drake said.

"Sure," Jack said.

Logan got the note out of his pocket.

Lin asked, "Can I see Quinn's note again, Logan?"

Logan gave the note to Lin.

Lin looked at the note. Then she gave it back to Logan.

"What should we do first?" Paige asked.

Lin said, "I know what we should do first. We should count how many times each letter is in the code."

"That's for sure," Jack said.

But then Paige looked at her watch.

Paige said, "We'll have to do that later. Lunch is almost over. We need to go. We can't be late for our next class."

"What am I going to do? I have to break the code," Logan said.

It wasn't really a big deal. But Logan wanted to date Quinn. So it was a big deal for him.

"Don't worry, Logan. We'll help you after school," Jack said.

"Yeah," Drake said.

"Where should we meet, Logan?" Paige asked.

"How about in front of my apartment?" Logan said.

"What time?" Paige asked.

"As soon as we get home, Paige," Logan said.

Willow said, "I can't, sorry. I have to work today."

Willow wanted to be a librarian. She loved books. And she worked at the town library some days after school and on some weekends.

"I can't meet then either. I have football practice," Drake said.

Drake was on the football team. He was the quarterback.

"What about the rest of you? Can you meet then?" Logan asked.

Lin said, "I'm sorry, Logan. I want to help. But I have to write a paper. And I must finish before I can help."

Logan looked at Jack and Paige.

Logan asked, "What about you two? Can you help me as soon as we get home?"

"You can count on me, Logan. That's for sure," Jack said.

Paige said, "And you can count on me, too. But there's one problem."

"What?" Logan asked.

"I'll be glad to try to help you break the code. But I'm not good at doing things like that," Paige said.

"Don't worry, Logan. I'm good at codes. And we'll break the code. That's for sure," Jack said.

Logan hoped Jack was right about that. But Logan wasn't sure.

# Chapter 7

Logan sat in front of his apartment. Jack and Paige were with him. All three had pencils and some paper. Logan had Quinn's note, too.

Logan had read the note many times. But he still didn't know how to break the code.

"What should we do first, Jack?" Logan asked.

"We should each have a copy of the secret message," Jack said.

"Then we should make some copies of the secret message first," Paige said.

Logan didn't want to write on the note. So he wrote it out again twice.

Then Logan asked, "What should we do next?"

"We need to make an ABC chart," Jack said.

They quickly wrote the ABCs on a sheet of paper.

"Now what?" Logan asked.

Jack said, "Now we should look at each letter in the code. And we should put a mark by that letter on our ABC chart."

Logan did that. But it took him a few minutes.

Then Logan asked, "Now what?"

"We should count how many times each letter is in the code. And then put that number by that letter on our chart," Jack said.

All three did that.

"Now what?" Logan asked.

Jack said, "Now we can break the code."

Jack made it sound very easy to do. But Logan knew it wouldn't be that easy to do.

"How do we break the code, Jack?" Logan asked.

Jack said, "When we write, we use some letters more than other letters. The letter we use most is *E*. The next letter we use most is *T*."

"Are you sure about that, Jack?" Paige asked.

"Yeah, Jack. Are you sure about that?" Logan asked.

"Yes. I read that in a book about codes," Jack said.

Logan was glad to hear it. Maybe Jack really did know how to break codes.

"We need to see which letter is in the code the most times. It might be an *E*," Jack said.

All three looked at their charts.

Paige said, "The code has thirteen *F*s. Maybe the *F*s are really *E*s."

"Put an *E* over each *F*. But we might have to change them later," Jack said.

They put an *E* over each *F*.

Then Logan asked, "Now what?"

"The code has nine *U*s and eight *P*s. Maybe the *U*s or the *P*s are really *T*s," Paige said.

"But which one is the *T*, Paige?" Logan asked.

Jack said, "We need to look at the words. We need to see if any words begin with a *U* or a *P*."

"Why?" Logan asked.

"Because *the* is the three-letter word we write most often. And *that* is the four-letter word we write most often. Both of them begin with *T*," Jack said.

Paige said, "Four words begin with a *U*. And only one word begins with a *P*."

"Yeah," Logan said.

Jack said, "The *U*s might really be *T*s. We can put a *T* over each *U*. But we might have to change that later."

The three quickly did that.

Then Logan said, "*UIF* must be the word *the*."

"So the *I* must really be an *H*," Paige said.

The three quickly put an *H* over each *I*.

But that didn't help Logan a lot. He still couldn't break the code.

"This code is too hard," Logan said.

"It's hard. And we'll break the code. But we just have to work some more on it," Paige said.

"Yes. We'll break the code. That's for sure," Jack said.

Logan thought the code was hard. But he wanted to work on the code some more. And he was glad his friends did, too.

# Chapter 8

All three looked at the secret message for a few more minutes.

Then Logan asked, "What should we do now?"

"We should try to guess what some of the words are. We can start with the first word," Jack said.

"Good idea, Jack," Paige said.

"Yeah," Logan said.

The three looked at the code.

Then Paige said, "I think *NFFU* is *meet*. And *NF* is *me*."

"Then *N* must be an *M*," Logan said.

The three put an *M* over each *N*.

"Now what?" Logan asked.

Jack said, "I think *UIFO* is *then*."

"I think you're right, Jack."

"So the *O* must be an *N*, Jack," Logan said.

The three put an *N* over each *O*.

Then Jack said, "I think I know how Quinn made the code."

"How?" Paige asked.

"Yeah. How?" Logan asked.

Jack said, "Look at the letters above *NFFU*. The *M* is the letter that comes before *N*. And *E* is the letter that comes before *F*."

"And *T* is the letter that comes before *U*," Logan said.

Jack said, "Now you can see how Quinn made the code. She wrote the next letter for each letter in the secret message."

Paige said, "You're right, Jack. That's what Quinn did."

Logan looked at the code. Then he said, "Yeah, Jack. That's what she did."

Now Logan knew how to break Quinn's code.

Logan wrote the letter that came before each letter in the code.

Then Logan could read Quinn's code.


MEET ME BEFORE SCHOOL. WE CAN MEET IN FRONT OF THE SCHOOL. WE CAN TALK ABOUT THE DATE THEN.


Logan said, "Now I know why Quinn got mad at me."

"So do I. You were talking to me before school. And you should have been talking to Quinn," Paige said.

"But that was because I didn't know how to break the code," Logan said.

"You can tell Quinn that, Logan. And

maybe she'll date you now," Jack said.

"I hope she will," Logan said.

Logan could hardly wait to tell Quinn he'd broken the code. Or maybe he would tell her that he and his friends had broken the code.

He hoped Quinn wouldn't be mad at him then. And he hoped she would date him.